Lilith's Haven

REAGAN ELLIS

ATROPA

A note from the author

Please note that the depiction of God in this story is fictitious, not the god you know but rather a representation of the systems in place to keep women and marginalized communities oppressed. Whether you blame a god for that oppression is your business. Additionally, this story mentions rape, murder, abuse, violence, assault, sexism, transphobia and other potentially triggering and sensitive subjects. Please take care of yourself and skip out on this book if it's not for you.

With so much love,
Reagan Ellis

for any woman who has ever felt the mud,

may you find your revenge

CHAPTER 1

A Quiet Porch

Nestled between the constellations, atop a cliff made of ever-flowing moonlight, sat a house full of dead women. It was on the porch of that very house that Eloise had the paralyzing realization that she herself was, in fact, a dead woman.

It wasn't the feeling that you'd expect, realizing you're dead. She did not feel terror or tragedy as she looked around the wooden porch and the ethereal nature beyond. All she found within herself was a quiet confusion, for Eloise could remember nothing about herself save the name she had been given.

One can't be sure what abnormality led her to the knowledge that she was dead. Maybe it was the nightshade growing up through her irises, or the hourglass she had been clutching to her breast, all the sand gathered and still at the bottom. But it was likely the apparition of an old woman standing in the arched doorway, beckoning Eloise in, and asking how she takes her tea.

As if in an afterlife trance, Eloise rose from her place on the floor and passed through the threshold. Though she wasn't aware of how her limbs felt sweeping across the floor, she was acutely aware of everything else, her senses seemingly heightened in her state of death. The stale air crackled with the distant hum of a record player spinning oldies. A smell holding the promise of pie coaxed her further into the candlelit foyer. The apparition gave her a warm smile from her spot in front of the overbearing staircase. On the landing above, a cat stretched in front of a stained glass window, bathing in the moonlight that cast a multicolored pattern on the floor. A grandmother clock struck a time that Eloise couldn't make out from her vantage point, the sound causing the cat to startle, leaping down the stairs and brushing past the white nightgown Eloise hadn't known she was wearing.

"Come, come!" The apparition said, starting down a narrow hallway lined with an equally narrow red carpet that barely covered the hardwood floors beneath. They came to a kitchen, warm with the heat of a freshly baked pie and a simmer pot of lavender. The pot sat adjacent to a black-and-gold-adorned teapot that matched the exterior of the house. Eloise took a seat at the small, round table in the middle of the room and looked to the windows that offered a stunning view of a thousand stars, close and distant.

"With honey," Eloise whispered, finally answering the question the apparition had asked on the porch. The old dead woman just giggled, preparing the two cups of tea. Eloise watched the woman as she worked, noticing how her dark skin glowed in the starlight, her curly hair framing her wrinkled face. She reached a high cabinet by way of her tippy toes, winking at Eloise as she pulled down a jar of honey. Those eyes held nothing but kindness and light, complimenting her blush-rose bathing robe.

Eloise knew the whole situation should have struck her as odd–the dead women moving about the kitchen and the fact that they shared that trait–but she felt an attitude of acceptance deep within her.

Joining Eloise at the table, the woman gave her a tight smile, handing the tea off.

"The pie will be done soon," The apparition said after Eloise had taken her first sip.

"I'm Bella. And this," she said, gesturing to the space around them, "is Lilith's Haven. Welcome, Eloise."

How did Bella know her name? Before Eloise had the chance to ask, Bella slid an envelope across the table. Eloise gave the envelope a questioning look before opening it, taking the letter out. In elegant handwriting, the letter served one message:

> Eloise,
>
> You are cordially invited to stay in our boarding house for as long as your healing heart desires. Welcome to the prologue of afterlife darling, I have no doubt that you will overcome all that's been done to you through the support of your newfound sisters. I'll be home for a visit soon.
>
> I'm forever regretful that I couldn't do more for you.
>
> All my love,
> Lilith

It was signed off with a black lipstick mark, the kiss of death herself. Eloise put the letter down, finding a slice of apple pie where the envelope had been. The realization washed over her again when she noticed that for the first time in her life, now afterlife, that her chest was neither rising nor falling. And she realized that it hadn't been for quite some time.

"Heaven or Hell?" Eloise demanded, no longer whispering. Bella only cocked her head, puzzled.

"Is this Heaven or Hell?" She was a bit more frantic this time.

"We exist beyond that binary." Bella's answer came out steady, rehearsed. "A sort of limbo, where you are free to mend your soul until you decide to join the world of the dead. It is offered to you based on the same merit that it's offered to our other residents: the manner in which you passed."

Passed. Passed. Passed. Eloise turned the word over and over like a coin in her mind, trying to make heads of it all. She knew she should feel unsettled, but was truly incapable of feeling anything other than shock.

"I'm the house mom," Bella continued. "While other spirits come and go, I stay here. A guide of sorts."

She took Eloise's hands in her own, her eyes growing serious and focused.

"Sweetie, do you remember how you died?"

Died. Died. Died. How had she died?

"It's okay, Eloise. A lot of women take time to remember. It's often the first step." She paused, sympathy written across her face, "The pie will help. As will sleep, time, and patience with yourself."

Yourself. Yourself. Yourself? Who was she? She had forgotten. Eloise caught a whiff of lavender that sent her mouth into a yawn for air that she no longer needed.

Eloise felt a rattling in her chest, thrashing to understand her situation. She was *dead*. Speaking with a *ghost*.

Bella seemed to recognize the tension, offering Eloise an escape, "Why don't I show you to your room?"

Seeing no other option and feeling a heavy exhaustion weighing down on her, Eloise followed Bella back down the narrow hallway and up the sturdy stairs. Her second walk through the house allowed her more time to notice the oil paintings hanging on every wall. Who was she?

They walked past a series of doors across from the railing that overlooked the staircase until they were before the last door, settled next to a small window. Bella sorted through the contents of her pocket; a button, a needle, a few small rocks, a compact mirror, and finally a key. She offered it to Eloise.

"Here," Bella said, "open what's now yours."

So she did.

CHAPTER 2

Lilith

My story varies from house to house, no two versions the same. Each recitation has left its own unique alteration on the tale: a claw mark, a stain, a lie, a kiss, or a jinx. The interpretations share only one truth: I would never willingly submit to a man.

Whether you believe I was banished for adultery, disobedience, or a stillborn life, I can guarantee that you neglect to know the paramount of my legend, the punishment beyond the walls of Eden, my curse.

For banishment from paradise was not enough for your vengeful god.

CHAPTER 3

Breakfast for the Dead

Eloise found the open layout and floral painting adorning the walls of her room at the end of the hall to be familiar, but her sleep had been restless nonetheless.

The dreamless night was so dark that Eloise had no choice but to confront the few memories that presented themselves in slow, entwining vignettes. She watched as she walked through the gardens of her parents' home in Kyoto. A glimpse into their life prior to immigration. Watched through her mind's eye as she progressed into a talented and accredited painter. She saw parts of her life shift into others–a ring sliding onto her left hand that went on to scoop her daughter into an embrace.

Eloise awoke to the calico house cat peering over her, tail whipping back and forth to some unheard rhythm.

Remembering made her feel hollow, a sensation that came with longing for something she could not return to. She wept for the glimpses of a life she could not truly recall, trying and failing to rationalize the concept of dying in her mind. It was a lonely feeling to not remember anyone, even herself.

She straightened the green silk sheets on her bed and noted a vase of nightshade on the bedside table; they were from her arrival the previous day. She went down to the kitchen, on the hunt for breakfast. Not that she needed it, she supposed. Routine, she had decided, would kick up her memory.

To her bemusement, Eloise found that the view from the kitchen had not changed. It was still dark out, save the shining stars.

She searched through cabinets, drawers, pantries, and a freezer box, but found nothing but cobwebs. She was about to head back upstairs to dwell on the idea that she might never have a bite of breakfast again when she heard a rich laugh coming from a part of the house she had yet to step foot in. Following the sound, she crossed the foyer to a new hall, this one considerably wider, with more lights to illuminate her walk. At the end of the hallway she found billowing white linen curtains that seemed to move in sync with the laughter she had used as her compass. They parted for her to enter.

"Eloise! You're just in time!" Bella chirped from her seat at the head of the long, ornately carved dining table. Jewel-toned silk table runners, candles, and flowers decorated any space that wasn't covered with the teeming amount of biscuits, pastries, fruit, and waffles.

The seven women at the table stopped their chatter to smile at Eloise. A redhead with rosy cheeks and an abundance of freckles tapped the empty space next to her in silent invitation. Eloise gave the woman a genuine grin and made her way to the seat.

"You must be Eloise! My name is Ansel." The redhead leaned in and gave Eloise a strong hug. It wasn't just the hug that was strong. Though she had a ghostly glow, Ansel herself looked as though she had spent a lot of time using her muscles before she died. Ansel's introduction was just the first in a cascading chain of names as the girls became acquainted with their new housemate.

Tala

Lulu

Advaita

Kali

Claudette

Each name felt like one her soul had been missing for a long, long time. She took in the sight of the ghostly dead women; they ranged from shade and shape, every feature unique, every presence perfect. It was the most beautiful thing Eloise had ever encountered. She tried to drink up every wrinkle, curve, and color of the group so that she might paint it when she had the chance. She knew she loved these people already. Her brain whispered each of their names over and over, folding them into a sacred space in her soul. The loneliness lessened in their presence, and a feeling of home teased at her unbeating heart.

She started by getting to know the people seated closest to her while the others continued their previous conversations. While all the girls had a somewhat transparent shine about them, their souls seemed well and alive. She learned that while living, Ansel had been a famous swimmer, earning prizes for her swiftness in the sea. Advaita had grown up in Jaipur, where she met her girlfriend. Advaita's retelling of their first encounter included consistently vulgar language that often sent those around her into roaring laughter. Lulu explained in a Southern voice that she had worked in a post office in Georgia but spent a good portion of her time volunteering at a center for senior citizens, giving lessons in ballroom dancing. She told them about growing up in the South with the sort of sarcasm that had Eloise hanging on every word.

They gorged on the decadent fruit and pastries, losing

track of whatever time the afterlife ran on. The stars outside seemed to glow brighter, laughter and warmth filled the heavy emptiness she felt in her deflated lungs, the type of sensation that can only come from a sort of sisterhood.

After a while Ansel got a dreamy look in her eye and announced, "I have an idea."

CHAPTER 4

Lilith

I remember mud. Slick between my fingers, hands splayed out on the ground, mimicking the position the rest of my body found itself in upon impact. The mud clung to my bare form, as thick and dirty as my disappointment in God. I remember mud splattered in my vision, mixing with the red I saw from the raw rage boiling inside of me when I looked up at Adam. He looked back at me like I was the mud, not seeing the human beneath.

I bet it's not the kind of story you'd expect to hear from the glorified paradise of your dreams. Your bound books of gold foil make you forget that it is still a garden, and just like everything else God designed, it is subject to filth if provoked. And I remember the filth, the mud, filling that space between my nails, hanging on my eyelashes, latching its irrevocable reputation to my name forever.

My own story has been told to me so many times that I no longer remember the truth. Did I lose a baby? Did I refuse to create one? I cannot remember, I only remember the mud that followed, an act of God's violence, certainly not his first. For what was the creation of man if not violent? To hurtle forged souls into a game with no context of the board, the rules, the risk. Only the promise of wrath should the game maker lose. What is the concept of rules to a pawn? I imagine it's about the same as the concept of a perfect god to an over-powerful being that enacts revenge in the first chapter of his book.

The mud stained me in a way that has passed down to every woman to follow me onto this Earth, branding us objects. Hit us. Spew your vituperation on us. Force us. Shove us to the ground. Torture us. Inject us with your venom. Abuse us. Capture us. Murder us. Why shouldn't they see the mud their highly coveted God covered the first of us with and follow in his footsteps?

When God cursed me in that mud, I was reborn. I closed my eyes and inwardly promised a curse of my own. And oh how the heavens shall split open and sing when God falls at the very hands he covered in mud.

I was sentenced to spend my immortal life as a grim reaperess.

I spend my existence collecting the souls of the fallen and taking them where they need to go. It's haunting work in more ways than one. Peace can be found in death, but more often than not I find myself before a soul that was tortured in its last moments. More often than not that soul is a woman who has died for being so. This is the nature of my curse.

Femicide is an invisible wildfire that threatens to swallow your world whole. And I watch. I weep unseen in the shadows of the rooms and streets and woods that backdrop the atrocities befallen your women. Each time I witness one, the suffering feels new, and I suffocate in the restraints that keep me from interfering. There is no greater pain.

It is my belief that women were designed with an extra corner or cubby of the soul, one that has the capacity to hold the pain that comes with knowing another woman's autonomy has been destroyed, a place that harbors the hurt like its own. At the foot of this cubby lies a fire that never ceases to burn, but sears and smokes when misogyny stokes the ever-angry flame. At the entrance you'll find a threshold designed to keep all the pain and heat in, until the soul is sweltering, with no escape.

I find that in the final moments of life, the only thing I can do is attempt to ease that pain. It's simple really, just ask their soul to tell you a story, for they all have one to share.

As I tell you my story, without the claw marks, stains, lies, kisses, or jinx, I too shall platform the songs sung in the moments before death. The stories the current residents of the haven had to tell.

CHAPTER 5

Soul stories: Who's afraid of monotony?

Advaita

What if I told you I was wrong? Three words I seldom permit to escape my lips, or even live within the chambers of my mind. But it seems that I have been wrong quite frequently these days, and I am getting better at admitting it, finding the bravery in failure. Love can change you like that.

It was Holika Dahan, and as my family danced around the glorious flames, I realized I might never tell the truth, forever cursed by my own damn ambitions. It was a web spun of my own devices, though I didn't realize it at the time.

I had boasted that fact since childhood to anyone who would listen: "I'm going to become famous and leave this city." Along with other proclamations of never falling in love or settling into the terrors of monotony. These were fully self-inflicted desires. Dreams I crafted out of fear that I wouldn't create a life worth living.

Everything changed when I met her. In the vibrant streets of Jaipur, under a cloud of primarily green Holi powder, her eyes met mine through twirling colors of people. I tried to look away, but the damage had been done. I was hers the moment I got close enough to notice the red powder that had been brushed across her cheeks and bridge of her nose.

She leaned in close and transferred some of that red onto me, introducing herself over the music and laughter, her name embedding itself into my heart: Meera.

We spent the rest of the day together singing and dancing and eating barfi until our stomachs hurt.

It really sucks, as you might imagine, to fall in love when you swore up, down, left, and right that you *never* would. It's a battle of pride and desire, ego and heart. But she was an unstoppable force of light who would throw her hands up to the sun and dance for it. She accepted my vulgar jokes with a soft laugh, replacing the reprimands I usually met with a featherlight love. She saw past the facade of my aspirations to the real me.

One day I tried to end things with Meera. I cried as I told her I needed to leave, to make something of my life. The pressure I had felt to be exceptional was unbearable.

She laughed and laughed, seeing through me in a way I never thought possible. "Advaita, what is it that you love? Not what you think you should love, not the armor you don to protect yourself from disappointment, but what is your passion?"

I didn't know how to answer the question. Ever since I was born I felt an incessant need to be great, whatever that means. To make waves in the world before it drowned me. I told everyone I wasn't interested in love to get in front of the fear that no one could ever feel that for me. I closed my eyes and focused on Meera's question. I saw the countryside of Rajasthan, the colors of Holi, the trees that bear fruit low enough to be handpicked by children. I saw Meera's smile after a particularly dirty joke and the intricate arches of Hawa Mahal during the sunset.

I opened my eyes and realized that I was wrong. When I thought of my future I no longer dreamed through the lenses of paparazzi cameras and planes to take me far away, but of something else entirely. Something so precious I didn't dare speak it out loud.

I was sitting before the fire of Holika Dahan when I decided it was time. Almost a year after meeting Meera I knew that my dreams had changed, and I was okay with that. I just had to swallow my pride and take the steps towards a life founded on genuine ambitions.

I was just about to tell my parents, admit that my dreams had changed, when someone took me here, to this dark place where not even her light could reach. I fear I'll never get to tell Meera that I love her. That she's taught me that it's okay for dreams to change. Especially when they change into something as beautiful as her.

CHAPTER 6

Water Lilies

Wearing nothing but the glow of the moonlight under them and the stars above, the women sprinted through the forest surrounding the haven. They laughed and howled as the wind whipped past them, acting as they might've their whole life had they not been forced into the confines of civility. Gone was the urge to conceal the body as though its only function was beauty.

They ran and ran until they at last beheld the inky waters of an indigo-tinted pond. The water was bracketed by blue, purple, and emerald foliage in the surrounding forest. The colors differed from what they had known on Earth, with barren, skeletal-looking trees and soft grass that appeared green or violet depending on how the starlight hit it. Water lilies bobbed in the water, greeting the women as they approached. Advaitia took a bounding leap before diving into the water. The others followed in after her. The girls splashed and swam, reborn in the smooth water.

"You just 'bout look like a mermaid!" Lulu gushed at Eloise. With her short blonde hair and plump form catching the starlight like that, Eloise thought she didn't look anything short of ethereal herself, more faerie than human. Though she supposed none of them were human. Not in the way they had once come to understand. Ghosts, spirits, but not humans. The thought didn't hurt, but it didn't bring her any sort of peace, either. She knew her soul couldn't fully rest until she remembered her last moments, what fleeting actions had sent her here, and who she had been prior.

Being around the women had helped her to remember certain things: her love of picking wildflowers, of rescuing animals, the gentle nature she had inherited from her mother. All those memories were overshadowed by the notion that the human version of her no longer existed.

Advaita dunked Eloise under the water, shaking her from her trance. The two came up in roaring laughter, sending water flying at each other. Eloise was immediately on offense, slithering under the surface and jerking Advaita's feet out from under her so she was submerged in the sweet-smelling water. They kept on the caper for a few minutes before tiring. Ansel and Lulu were doubling over with laughter by the time they were through.

"Glad we could be of entertainment." Advaita rolled her eyes, flicking water their way.

"Ansel, why don't you tell us one of your *stories*," Lulu requested. Eloise leveled her questioning look, some suspicion around the way Lulu said stories.

Under her breath Lulu said, "She can be a bit"–a pause–"outlandish at times. It's why we love her."

So Ansel began weaving an epic tale of her supposed encounter with a sea dragon. She had gotten lost during one of her swim races until a boat of ruthless pirates found her. They offered her a trade: if she could discover the infamous sea dragon's name, they'd take her home. Ansel recited her mythic journey to find the beast, refusing to yield how exactly she forced the name from the creature. At last, when the entirety of the group's attention was on Ansel and her words, she revealed what they had all wanted to know:

"And the raging bitch-dragon's name... was Advaita!"

Laughter erupted from everyone's lips, the loudest of all being Advaita. Once settled, Lulu joined Tala and Claudette in a song, mesmerizing and enchanting everyone. Their chorused voices were unlike anything Eloise had heard on Earth–further confirmation that she was no longer there.

As conversation flowed, Eloise wandered off and found herself being drawn to a cluster of water lilies by the deep end of the water's edge. She ran a finger over the delicate petal and admired its pale coloring. Before she could react, the pistil in the center rolled over into a cloudy emerald eyeball. It blinked once before its stem shot through the water, gripped Eloise's wrist, and dragged her down, down, down.

Fear rang between Eloise's ears when she beheld a mirror at the bottom of the pond. The lily released its grip and Eloise was relieved to realize that the flower spirit had no intention of harming her, just a desire to lead her to the discarded mirror. She swam towards it, not needing breath to stay under.

But when she got to the mirror, it was not her reflection she came face to face with, but rather her death.

CHAPTER 7

Lilith

I hadn't cried when Eloise Kimura died.

No, I was crying long before I gathered every shattered bit of Eloise's soul and escorted it past the thin shiny veil that divides the living and the dead.

Death had hung in the air like an unanswered question for days, frequently summoning me to the room before it was truly time to take her soul. I watched as Eloise clung to her life, as blood was drawn, and as she was abused again and again. I bore witness to the horrors I had encountered in so many women before Eloise, horrors I would encounter again long after. I always stayed with them, even if they couldn't see me. It was an act of solidarity as well as an act of rebellion against the God who ignored the calls for help, for him.

Eloise had a light inside of her, as all souls did. And I wept as it went out, the last words Eloise would ever hear still echoing through the walls.

"You little bitch."

CHAPTER 8

Simmer

Eloise found herself seated around a blue bonfire later that night. The heat worked towards melting the feeling of sharp icicles that had been stabbing at her chest since her encounter with the mirror. It showed her very little, just fragmented images of her death, never allowing the perpetrator to come into focus. She was left with the knowledge that she had met a violent end. And as they sat around the fire she learned that all the women of Lilith's Haven had died in that horrible manner.

To put it plainly, Eloise felt anger. Anger that her daughter would have to live without a mother ate away at her. Anger that she would never get to teach her kin how to French braid that same way her mother had taught her, and her mother before that. Anger that her final piece of art would sit forever unfinished and that her career would be stained with the mystery and shock surrounding her death rather than defined by her art. Anger that the man had gotten away with it and that his mother wouldn't know to look at her son and feel shame and outrage.

"Tomorrow," Tala said from Eloise's right, "we will begin

taking turns to help you remember your life. We divided into groups of two that will take you to do something that helped us remember when we were in your position." Eloise didn't feel up to the task, wishing to stew in bed and never gain another painful memory. When Eloise didn't respond Tala decided to change the subject.

"You know, when the mirror in my bedroom tried to show me something for the first time, I got so scared that I threw it off the wall." Tala let out an endearing snort, her freckles bunching up with the action. Her reddish-brown skin wrinkling around her light-brown eyes. "So, you're handling it better than me."

"My God, Eloise. She threw the mirror into the wall that separates our bedrooms," Lulu claimed while smiling and nodding disapprovingly at Tala. "I thought I was dying all over again!"

"Oh, you did not!" Tala insisted. "You're just jealous that Eloise's first encounter with an afterlife mirror was semi-aquatic, and yours was sweeping up my broken one."

"I guess this does make you, like, six percent cooler than me." Lulu winked at Eloise, who smiled despite herself and replied with a question.

"Do all mirrors in the afterlife do that?"

"Only when they feel like it," Lulu scoffed, her twang especially sharp.

"I've been here the longest," Tala started, "and the best advice I can give you is not to drive yourself crazy trying to figure out how everything works here. I mean we're living on a cliff made of *moonlight*."

It made sense to Eloise that Tala had been there the longest. She had an air of control and confidence to her; she carried herself like a leader.

"How long have you been here?" Eloise asked Tala.

"Two years."

"Two–two years? I thought we could leave whenever we wanted to."

"We can. I just wanted to meet you before I left." Tala's lips formed a sly grin, emphasizing the idea that she was in complete control of her mannerisms, her life, and her story. Her reply confused Eloise. Had she known Eloise was going to die? Why would she want to meet her?

"Hush up!" Lulu urged. "You're opening a door to questions we are not allowed to answer until her memory is back! You'll drive poor Eloise crazy as a betsy bug."

But Eloise had always been patient, and Lulu's implication that answers would eventually come was enough for her. She felt ready to take on whatever the girls had in store for her tomorrow.

CHAPTER 9

Soul Stories: Bless her heart

LULU

Lordy, Lordy where to start? I guess we should probably start where I started, with my momma. The very woman that didn't make a fuss when at six years old I prayed—out loud at the dinner table—for the good Lord to please make me a girl. The woman didn't so much as sigh; I doubt her heart even skipped a beat. She simply stood up, smoothed her dress out, and ignored my enraged father as she offered me her manicured hand.

Being in the local dress store was the first time I ever felt comfortable. The lighting was disorientating, and I 'bout broke a sweat trying to ignore the hate spewing from the gossipin' hens who clearly had nothing better to do with their time as they whispered *That poor mother, bless her heart* and, *That boy's about a half a bubble off plumb, God save him.* But I just played pretend they weren't talking about us and went about my fashion show business. When my momma nearly bought out all the little girl's dresses they had in stock, suddenly those commission hens were all pearly whites and peaches.

The drive back home was less pearly whites and peaches.

No music was permitted on the ride back, which was odd, since Momma loved to belt it in the car if the right song came on at the right time. She said she needed my full focus. I was to enter my room via the window, which was no biggie for me because I slept on the first and only floor and always kept the window open to feel the breeze at night. From there I was to take my backpack and fill it with all of my favorite things, and most importantly I was to sit tight in my room til Momma came to get me, no matter what I heard. At the time it sounded an awful lot like a game, and I was ready to play.

Right before we pulled into the long, dusty driveway, my momma asked me a very important question. She asked with her voice that dripped with Southern honey, accent mirror to my own,

"Well, I suppose a beautiful girl such as yourself needs a beautiful name to fit. What'll it be darling?"

Her eyes met mine in the rearview mirror. I felt my cheeks flush pink as my mind desperately tried to grasp for anything slightly feminine. I looked down at the baby-yellow dress I had been clutching since we left the shop and read the tag: "Lulu's Dresses." And that was that.

As you might have suspected, the sit-tight-no-matter-what-you-hear-game was no game at all–rather something that I would reflect on in therapy all those years later. But in the end, I won. I sat tight until Momma came into my room with a swollen eye and once again offered me her hand.

The next twelve years of my life can be summed up in one word: lost. It was hard for my momma to find work, and even harder to keep my assigned gender a secret during those initial years. But even as my golden hair grew out to my shoulders, and my body filled out to something soft, round, and womanly, my momma's free spirit never transformed. She never became stagnant, and I had no option but to follow her lead. We traveled all over the country, never staying in the same spot for more than a year. The thing about moving a lot is that you 'become familiar with adapting. Always being the new girl meant I became very good at talking to people very fast. Lord knows no one was going to make friends for me.

It was my honed people skills that I utilized when I approached Jeremiah at the bar one day after a shift at the post office to introduce myself. He asked me where I was from, and I told him nowhere and everywhere.

This led to the question that has haunted me my entire life: "Army brat?"

I smiled sweetly, "Just a regular brat."

And poor Jere, all the way from Massachusetts, was not yet immune to a woman's Southern charm, causing him to fall madly in love with me. It couldn't be helped really. Inevitable even.

He didn't care that I was trans. And a drink led to a date led to cheesy jokes and walks home and a first kiss while slow dancing in the porch light, all building up to the highly coveted L-word, and the grand finale: moving in together.

I had gotten used to never feeling settled. I had become accustomed to building a home within myself when the physical world couldn't provide one. Home was knowing that I had myself, no matter what. Even when my soul didn't feel at home in my body, and my body didn't feel at home in that month's apartment, I learned how to make a place out of my existence. I was at peace with that. Comfortable, even–but moving in with him was truly understanding what it is to be able to go home. It was a relief like I had never known.

We fell into a symphonic pattern of packing lunches for each other and sharing a quick kiss at coffee, throwing dirty clothes into the same hamper, and making the same bed. And for a while I allowed myself to live in that sweet bliss. Until I remembered that everything can go away.

I loved working at the post office, I loved living in Georgia, and I loved Jeremiah. I suddenly had a lot to lose.

People often confuse the concept of stability with permanence. It comes from a fear of change, this idea that in order to feel secure in a feeling you have to make it last forever. Rationally, we know this isn't the case, but if there's one thing love takes away, it's common sense.

My fear of losing it all overrode the logical part of my brain. I felt as though my life was a towel on the beach, and I had to pin it down lest it fly away with the wind before I could catch it.

In the end I decided that I had to be the one to ruin my life before anyone else got the chance to.

I rebuilt the home within myself and left.

CHAPTER 10

Lilith

My first assignment was the type of heartbreak that moves you to creation. I was tasked to collect the life of an old woman named Belladonna. Belladonna had been her village's storyteller. Her age had anointed her with all the famous tales, as well as a few of her own invention. She tended a garden and never deigned to marry. The terms asexual and aromantic did not exist when she was alive, so they labeled her spinster. She just laughed at the supposed insult and went about growing the flowers in her garden and the minds of the youth through the power of stories and imagination that she had been born with. She was seldom cross, but almost always stern, although her temperament did not matter in the end. Nor did her passions or quirks. None of it mattered to the man who slit her throat, spilling her life onto the newly bloomed roses the night I took my first soul.

I remember finding it difficult to sort out her soul in the light of the moon, both the same shining and glorious color. Both fleeting as the day dawned.

"Why are you crying?" she asked me gently. The question

made my tears come faster. This woman, soul as bright as the moon, smiling down at me after just being murdered. She had appeared behind me as I set about my work. This was the first and only time this would happen. Every other soul that died from violence stayed unconscious until awaking on the front steps of the house, and more often than not could barely recall their names upon waking up. Souls that met a peaceful death were always conscious, eager to see what the afterlife had to provide for them.

"Why are you smiling?" I sniffled.

"Because it would appear my soul has left behind a flower."

Indeed. The pure magic of Belladonna's essence, along with the wrathful tears of a woman fallen, had created the world's first-ever deadly nightshade, Atropa belladonna. It sprouted up where Bella had fallen– another abnormality that would never come to pass again. I didn't know it then, but the plant would be the key to everything. As would the woman who inspired it. Following every woman's life I collected, from their soul a deadly nightshade would grow.

Bella held me as I sobbed. I explained my story to her, and she held it with the care of the storyteller she was, regarding it as sacred. She asked me to take her to my home.

I had been given a slice of the sky, the part where the moonlight gathered and flowed over into a cliff, complete with its own flora and fauna. It was here that Bella confided in me,

"I'm not yet ready to join the dead. Would it be all right if I stayed here with you? Just for a little?"

Our friendship blossomed in time with the nightshade we had planted. And what a gorgeous thing it was, to know and be known without restraint or judgment.

Creating the Haven wasn't really a decision we made. Just a slow-burning process of building a large house in case any other soul I collected wanted a place to stay. When I went to collect my next life, I found that many did. And it wasn't just a haven for the women who had died, but a place for me to rest with them. To share our pains and heal with each other when I wasn't out collecting. Bella, to my surprise, stayed. She is free to leave at any time, to join the afterlife, but I can't imagine she will. She finds joy in helping the ghosts process and heal, helping them to rediscover and redefine their stories, and allowing themselves to make room for new ones.

CHAPTER 11

Braids

Lilac-tinted liquid fell from the star-freckled sky as Eloise followed Advaita, Lulu, and the house cat down the front steps of the porch where she had awoken and into the mooncliff mud. Eloise leaned down to brush the calico creature, noting its unique eyes.

"What's the cat's name?" Eloise asked.

"That is not a fucking cat," Advaita stated, leveling at the creature a distrusting glare. The cat rubbed up against Advaita's ankles in return, much to her dismay.

"Her name is Orella, only Lilith knows what she truly is," Lulu answered.

"What do you mean she's not a cat?" Eloise said.

"She might be a cat, but at the very least she's a magical cat. She changes her appearance depending on her mood. Y'all would do well to avoid her when she's striped. I learned that the hard way," Lulu replied.

"So have we considered that maybe there is just more than one cat here? And you're all just assuming it's the same one?" Eloise joked.

"Nah," Advaitia said. "It's always got those same creepy-ass eyes. One blue and one green."

Eloise followed the girls over hills of moonlight backdropped by stars, watching as the lilac rain let up into a light mist. They eventually came upon a field of wildflowers and plants, the likes of which Eloise had never encountered.

"I thought this place might help you bring some of your memories back 'round. It helped me," Lulu said gently. Eloise surveyed the two women before her. Lulu was wearing a white linen sundress, displaying her round form. She was bright and glowy with two dimples and a blonde bob. Advaita was all legs in her black silk slip. In her little time here, Eloise had never seen the woman wear any expression besides the mischievous one. It permanently lived on her brown skin.

"What did you remember here?" Eloise asked.

"Oh a lil bit of this and that", Lulu said, brushing the question off in order to focus on Eloise. "Mainly how delightful and lovely I am." She batted her eyelashes, causing Advaita to laugh. Both women lowered themselves to the ground. Orella nudged Lulu's knee before settling into her lap.

"Let's start with facts you know," Advaita prompted when Eloise joined them in the blades of moonlight-colored grass, her green skirts bunching around her criss-crossed legs.

"My name is Eloise Kimura. I am a painter. I am twenty-eight years old. My parents are from Japan, but I grew up in Massachusetts, and I have a daughter. A beautiful, four-year-old daughter." She tried not to let her voice crack over this fact. "And I cannot remember her name." Eloise had tried and tried to remember, scanning her brain for constants and vowels that felt like home. Lulu reached out a comforting hand and placed it on Eloise's knee. "You will," she said with a certainty that matched the determination in her eyes.

"What can you remember about her? Let's start with that," Advaita suggested.

"I know she loves the sun and princesses. I know she was really excited to learn how to braid hair, and I was even more excited to teach her." Eloise said, nervously picking at the grass.

"You know," Lulu said, "I never learned how to braid. Could you teach me now while we talk? Maybe it will help." Eloise nodded and beckoned Advaita to sit in front of her in the iridescent grass. Eloise sat up on her knees and began demonstrating the best way to section hair into three parts. How to cross this lock of hair over that and back again. Lulu listened intently while Advaita faked pain when Eloise tugged on her hair.

As Eloise weaved the hair together, she felt some things coming back to her. The laughter of her closest friend, the best places to hike, her wedding dress, though she could not recall the groom. Most exciting, she thought, was remembering her favorite color: green.

It hurt her to only view snapshots of her life, and she begged her brain to focus on the details of a grainy memory. She finished Advaita's braid and sat before Lulu so she could try the style in Eloise's hair. Eloise had shorter hair than Advaita so the process would take less time.

"I can see that it pains you," Advaita said.

"Absolutely not. Lulu is doing a great job and I'm not nearly as tender-headed and over dramatic as you." Eloise said, her voice full of lighthearted teasing.

Advaita rolled her eyes and smiled. "Not the braiding process—the pain of trying to recall yourself and your life." She took Eloise's hand in her own. "I know that pain in my bones. We all do from when we first arrived, but I promise you'll remember, with time."

Eloise braced before saying what she hadn't wanted to

admit out loud. "But isn't it worse, to remember and not return?" The thought made her feel cowardly and selfish, to let the people of her life slip away with her memories of them.

Advaita gave her a sad smile and a squeeze of their joined hands, "A little, but we will be here for that mourning as well."

Eloise thought back to why they were all there.

The manner in which you died Bella had said. All these women too had gone through what she felt now. She was grateful to Lulu and Advaita for walking her out to the wild-flowers, if only to remember her favorite color.

"What about remembering death itself? I only remember the pain right now, not the full context." The question made Advaita's face turn grim.

"Rage like you have never known, Eloise." She shuddered. "But in time, you will come to learn of the plan."

Lulu finished the braid, receiving praise for how impressive it was for a first try. The girls lay back on the ground and watched the constellations, Orella curled up against Eloise's shins.

"What kind of plan?" Eloise asked into the darkness.

"Revenge," Lulu said flatly.

Advaita laughed.

CHAPTER 12

The greenhouse

Eloise had spent the rest of the afternoon getting to know Lulu, Advaita, and herself. While Advaita told dirty jokes that had Eloise laughing harder than ever, Lulu gathered flowers to work into Advaita and Eloise's braids, and in turn, they tucked some into Lulu's short mane, flowers glowing amid the golden hair.

When the lilac rain had once again picked up, more rapid and intense this time, the three ran back to the house, laughing and squealing over the demise of their newly done hair. Orella had disappeared into thin air the second a crack of thunder shuddered her whiskers.

As soon as Advaita, Eloise, and Lulu stepped foot into the foyer of the house, the others were there, howling with laughter over their drenched appearance and urging them to the dining room so they could eat.

. . .

Bella claimed that it was her duty as house mom to provide entertainment post dinner and played them a few songs on a dusty piano before Eloise retired to bed.

She slept for about two hours before a blinding glow illuminated her entire room, sourced from the mirror on the wall opposite her bed. Dread and excitement filled her stomach as she prepared to see another memory. Instead, the light condensed down into a small, floating object. Eloise threw off her covers and grabbed the lit candle at her bedside before padding across the room. She found a golden key perched in the air. It glowed, beckoning her with an invisible force. Eloise plucked it from the air, observing an engraving of a flower along the sides when her door swung open on the high-pitched squeak of a hinge. Eloise was not startled to see a black cat sitting before the threshold, tail going back and forth, eyes revealing its identity to be Orella. The feline abruptly stood and turned towards the hallway. Eloise did not hesitate to follow the swishing tail out of the room.

Down the hall and down the stairs they went; candles mounted to the walls worked to cast their shadows on the floor. The dark figures followed them, copying their every move.

Orella silently led the ghostly woman out of the house, past the field of wildflowers, and into the oddly colored forest they went, around the pond, and deeper still into the forest until Eloise came face to face with a greenhouse of thick, dark-green glass. With a nudge at her heels from Orella, she tried the door to find it locked. She pulled the key from the pocket in her nightdress and unlocked it.

. . .

Just before she could step into the greenhouse, she shot up in her bed at the sound of Ansel's hearty laugh from down the hall. A dream. But she knew without a doubt that the greenhouse was not just something she dreamed up, but real. Truly on this mooncliff, and she needed to find it.

Up and out of her bed, she removed the mirror from the wall, and a golden, flower-engraved key promptly fell out from under it. Eloise picked the key up and turned back to her bed, where she found a black cat, one eye blue and one green, smiling at her.

CHAPTER 13

Soul stories: Mad Woman

Kali

My life on Earth could be defined by four things: my love of dance, my obsession with horror movies, my drive for justice, and the Nobel Peace Prize.

I grew up dancing, using it to take breaks from the hard parts of life and just *be*. Leap when I felt like screaming, spin when I felt like crying, dance when I felt like dying. A feeling I would become familiar with.

To be born with a tender heart is to live with the almost guaranteed destiny of dying with a bitter one. I came into this world with wide eyes and an even wider heart. It has always been my nature to care. Justice is a constant in the forefront of my mind. Acting as a feminist before I knew what the word meant, wearing my Swahili name like a badge of honor.

.   .   .

I've always been told the same seven words: *You are the strongest woman I know.*

I didn't understand it when I was little. Though a talented dancer, I certainly was not the most physically strong. Never did the most pull-ups in PE and never won any playground races. I hadn't survived anything tragic or overcome a trauma out of the normal, so it wasn't a compliment on my perseverance. It wasn't until I was older that I understood that the strength they were referring to was my character. My confidence when I call out bigotry, my fearless opinions that never soften in the face of opposition. My unapologetic empathy, and drive to lead even when my role in society didn't teach me that leadership was something a woman of color could do.

My bookshelves are lined with dance trophies and books gifted to me about prominent women throughout history, feminist theory, and girls who changed the world. All the first pages hold the same type of note, always a *Happy Birthday/Merry Christmas/Happy Kwanzaa* followed by the words, *to the strongest woman I know*!

It's funny, really, how a title can haunt you. To some in my life I'm a trailblazer, to others I'm too loud and take up far too much space.

The title never dampened the need to fix the world that was fastened deep within me. I protested wars, raised funds for the hungry, escorted girls into the abortion clinic to protect them from hecklers, and danced through it when everything became too loud. Eventually I found my greatest passion of all: journalism.

. . .

I was about four years into being a journalist when I noticed the darkness that had begun to grow in me. It had started far earlier, but I had been blind to it. When you make an effort to see all the wrong in the world, to recognize others' pain like it's your duty, you begin to feel a bit mad. When you're screaming at the world to care, begging the people in power to do something, anything, you go from the strongest woman they know to the craziest. The angriest. Which is ironic when you never wanted to be strong, never wanted to be angry–you just wanted the world to change. But that's not what they see. They see the big headlines with big words and use the sound of the world burning as background noise. Is it so wrong that I started wanting them to burn too? Might as well become as crazy and as angry as they see me. Become the bitch they called me.

I was on the precipice of burnout when I took on a passion project, a piece dedicated to the art of dancing, focusing especially on dancers in war zones and how they kept their craft alive. It was the completion of this work that resulted in my nomination for the Nobel Peace Prize.

But in the end my strength couldn't save me, and I'll never know if I did win that award.

CHAPTER 14

Lilith

A few years after the founding of Lilith's Haven, an oracle died. Upon receiving Bella's invitation to enter the house, the oracle opted for a walk through the nature surrounding our home instead. None had ever chosen this before. Bella wrote to me, requesting I return to the house as soon as possible. And as she had never asked this of me, I came home immediately. It was a day of firsts.

The oracle had one eye of emerald green and one of a frosty blue, both blind. I found her running her hands through our garden of nightshades. The plants we'd collected, with permission, from the women whose souls grew them.

"Lilith," she said, without turning around to greet me. "You do not yet know the power you hold when you grasp these berries, but I do. I see." She tilted her head back and howled a laugh. "Do you know that Satan has claimed credit for these stunning plants you and yours have made? But I always knew.

These are crafted by the vengeance of a woman scorned in mud and smote by God." At this, I smiled, ready to reply. Before I had the chance, she cut in.

"An act of vengeance will fertilize these plants and secure their poison to the highest level. A level that not even the creator of the world could survive. It cannot be you, Lilith, who enacts this revenge. It comes with the risk of damnation for all the flower bearers should you not pull off your part of the plot."

With that, the oracle vaporized into stardust and took a new form. I smiled and thought of the mud.

CHAPTER 15

Soul stories: What is a body?

Tala

What is a body? An anatomist will tell you it's the physical structure of an organism, composed of tissue, blood, and organs, a miracle of genetics and biology. A spiritualist will preach that it's a vessel to hold the soul and guide you through the human experience. My therapist said it's a part of yourself to accept with neutrality, but a younger version of myself understood that my body was growing, like the rest of the world around me.

It is my belief that there isn't a relationship in the world that compares to that of a child's connection to nature, and the understanding that their body is just another facet of it. Everything outdoors holds the potential for fairy-tale magic: the flowers are there to shelter the pixies from the rain; trees in the forest stand tall like a fortress to protect a hidden castle; and if you look closely, you can see a mermaid going out with the tide. For me, nothing equated to the feeling of absorbing the warmth of the sun on my skin and of making the waves my home until sunset.

My love for the ocean started where everything did for me: my sisters. Our parents had packed us up for a day trip to the beach, where we basked in the light and manipulated the sand into our own inventions. We ate sandwiches and chips and laughed in the salty, heavy air without a care in the world. Nothing compared to the feeling of diving into the waves with my sisters, picking out what color our mermaid tails would be. Sharing secrets beneath the brilliant blue sky. Proclaiming our love of the sea and feeling the ocean's kiss in response.

This adoration of the ocean was ripped away when my mind began to resent my body.

When did my subconscious begin to internalize beauty standards? Was it the animated princesses I looked up to, with waists slimmer than their heads? Was it the photoshopped magazine covers that sat at my eye level while my mom checked out our groceries for the week? Maybe it was my best friend scrutinizing the way I looked in my first bikini. I can still feel the sting of when the boys I considered to be friends began rating the very girls they grew up with, assigning numbers to our names based on our looks. The sisterhood and friendships I had grown up with were forced into a competition.

. . .

Just like that, at nine years old, I began punishing myself for not having the body of a fully grown woman with surgeries and photo touch-ups. My body became an ordinary object that I was determined to mold into a golden prize. Crunches and cutting meals before I hit double digits. My perception got warped, I couldn't tell what was real in the reflection. I was diagnosed with body dysmorphia before I got my first period.

My condition worsened for years. All I saw when I looked at myself was an outline around me, a cookie-cutter shape of what I had convinced myself I needed to look like. I began missing school; I didn't want other people to have to see what I saw in the mirror each morning. Sometimes the sight of myself would cause a physical reaction: shaking, loss of breath, or involuntarily throwing up.

The ocean. My bone-deep insecurities outweighed my desire for what had once felt like home. I couldn't stomach making my body vulnerable to others' judgment. I didn't want to give my brain more images of better bodies to weaponize against myself.

I had lost touch with the reality of the body, and in turn, lost my connection with nature. Nature and the body are undeniably interconnected. The veins of fall leaves like the veins in my arms. Unsymmetrical beauty in roses like that of a parent's face. Seashells that match the hue of your first love's eyes.

My body dysmorphia persisted, but with it bloomed a love for healing. I dreamed of becoming the first doctor in my family.

. . .

Medical school is expensive, and I lived in California, so when the opportunity arose, I didn't think that the repercussions of taking a modeling job to pay for my education would outweigh the benefits.

Agencies told me that they loved my "exotic look." I'm Native American, not exotic at all, though they never seemed to care when I said that.

As my modeling career grew, my mental health declined. I saw the side by sides of my body, the original and the airbrushed. I overheard some photographers call me ugly while dodging the sexual advances of others. All the while the question rang in my head: What is a body?

I began healing when I remembered what I already knew; the body is another facet of nature. That's why we can catch snowflakes on our tongues during those blue winter nights. It is also why our legs can climb the old oak tree across the street. Why we live by the rules of the sun and the moon, using the core of the Earth to guide our compass. Why we can hear the song of a bird and sing one back, feel grass between our toes on a hot July day, and know with a deep sense of resilience that everything is going to be okay.

It's how other people have channeled the stars to be a light on my darkest day until I can return the favor. The greatest gift the body can give: the ability to help others.

. . .

It was with this answer that I finally began to enjoy modeling, not caring what others had to say. I took back the narrative of my body, refusing to work with editors who did insane photoshop on my already perfect body. Perfect simply because it existed.

Unfortunately, my love for my body and myself did not save me from the man who took one look at me and decided I owed him something.

I wonder if I would've been a good doctor.

CHAPTER 16

Six wings

The next day it was Kali and Tala's turn to help Eloise regain her past. She met them by the pond, trying her best to keep her mind from wandering back to her dream and the greenhouse that had been. Eloise was feeling extra sick of not being able to recall her life and was ready for whatever the women had to throw at her on that day.

"If I had to describe the feeling of trying to regain my memories," Kali said, "I would say I felt trapped."

Eloise nodded solemnly, knowing the feeling well. She was trapped somewhere deep in her brain, where memories would glow under the crack of the door, fickle and weak. Try as she might to open the door, she was trapped.

Kali's dark skin stood out against her yellow sweater. Her hair, typically down, was in bantu knots that revealed her high cheekbones, which rounded like rosebuds when she smiled.

"And if I had to name the opposite of feeling trapped, I

would name the feeling of flying." Those rosebud cheeks made an appearance, punctuating the sentence.

"Do we have a lot of planes here in Lilith's Haven?" Eloise quipped, and the two women laughed.

"We have something better." Kali gestured towards Tala.

"Ourselves. Ever wonder what it would be like to fly, Eloise?" Tala asked.

"Of course," Eloise said this like it was a basic human instinct to look to the skies and wish.

"What if I told you, that here, it is possible." Tala's eyes twinkled.

"Honestly," Eloise answered, "I'd believe you."

"Good." It was Tala's turn to smile, her light-brown skin in contrast to the pink hue of her lips. "Believing is really all you need."

And before Eloise could even respond, Tala transformed into a beautiful turquoise-feathered eagle, taking off towards the sky with a beautiful pealing call. Eloise stared after her in astonishment.

"H-how?"

"Pick any flying animal and envision yourself in the sky. That really all there is to it." And with that Kali winked before forming into an elegant flamingo and taking flight.

Stunned, Eloise looked up at the two birds waiting for her above. She closed her eyes, and pictured an emerald swallowtail butterfly, imagining what it would feel like to let go. She manifested as a much larger version of the swallowtail in order to keep up with the birds, and flapped up to where they were waiting.

With the power of her mind and body, Eloise had transformed. She felt like she was on top of the world, and began ascending upwards to that point.

Together they soared, the eagle, the flamingo, and the butterfly, through the permanently night-set sky and over the light of the mooncliff. They playfully bumped into each other, and Kali was right–for the first time since dying, Eloise felt free from the trap of memory.

They flew low to the ground, looking at flowers of every color, then shooting back up to trace the constellations with the tips of their wings. The breeze was a song beneath their wings as they started to land, but Eloise stumbled as an epiphany hit her.

Thoma.

Her daughter's name was Thoma.

CHAPTER 17

Soul Flowers

Falling asleep was getting harder as time passed, and Eloise grew impatient with herself and her lost memories.

This night, Eloise instantly knew it was a dream. She was *inside* the greenhouse, which was filled with only one type of plant; nightshade. She went to run her hand over the plants, but her fingers slipped through like she had reached out for a mirage, further confirming that she was in a dream. She walked down aisles and aisles of the poison until she found Orella in the back right corner. Tonight Orella had taken on a snow-white coat, and when the cat leapt down from her spot among the flowers, Eloise saw that the last slot for nightshade was empty.

She retraced her steps, finding that no other spot in the greenhouse was barren, no other nightshade missing. In fact, the plants had begun to entwine together, holding each other up and supporting saggy leaves or drooping stems. Eloise swore that if she closed her eyes and listened intently, she could hear a sort of harmony or hum coming from the belladonna.

"Soul flowers," a voice called. Eloise startled, looking up to find a woman the color of moonlight, wrapped in black smoke that blended in with her hair, watching her from across a row of nightshades.

It was Lilith. Though they had never met, she knew it was her with certainty. Eloise moved towards her, so many questions bubbling beneath the surface. When Lilith reached out, Eloise expected the hand to pass through her dreaming form, but it didn't. Her hand latched solidly onto Eloise's cheek before tucking a stray lock of hair out of her face.

"You beautiful girl," Lilith said. "You deserved so much more."

Eloise woke up with a tear falling down her face.

CHAPTER 18

Soul Stories: Swan girl

Ansel

I must have been a storyteller in my past life. The way I see the world through a certain fiction that worries those around me. I get paid to swim in races but recite my victories in the form of glittering quests. I fear abominable monsters that others cannot see, and listen to the secrets of the flame sprites until the whole blue town calls me mad. My parents wanted a swan to inspire ballets but got one suited to write them.

I must have been a knight in my past life, the way I dream of dragons and crowns. How I was built to wield a sword with the song of ferocity in my heart. The way loyalty courses through my blood, always on the defense. Always willing to fight for what I love. My parents wanted a swan to protect and got one suited to guard them instead.

. . .

I must have been the wind in my past life. The way I rattle the otherwise unfettered ocean. Slicing through waves and jetting against the current. I was born on the shore and learned to swim in the embrace of the Atlantic. My poor parents wanted a sane swan but instead found themselves with one that preferred the sea to the pond. The chaos to the calm, novelty to monotony, solitude to the flock.

The ocean takes me and my strength and my stories and treats me the same way it would treat that sane swan. The ocean holds no bias. The ocean says nothing of paranoid women, the same way it would say nothing of a lonely man. My parents wanted a daughter they could name Swan but took one look at the fire in my hair and in my eyes and knew the name would not do at all.

But maybe they got a Swan after all, just not the one they envisioned. I wonder if that's what they will say at my funeral, or if they will keep singing that old song.

CHAPTER 19

Lilith

The way I went about my immortal life was different after my conversation with the oracle. After she left the greenhouse I found a note where she had been.

100,006.

100,006 nightshades were required to poison God.

I was going to need some more greenhouses.

Every soul I collected was a heartbreak, but also an opportunity to obtain the plant their soul had made, should they choose to donate it to us and our cause. As Bella and I healed the women we brought to the Haven, we worked towards a permanent solution: Taking out the enabler of violence and abuse.

CHAPTER 20

Soul Stories: Hopeless romantic

CLAUDETTE

It's like I was born to be a spy when you think about it. My mother is French, my father is Spanish, and we live in the US of A. Meaning I speak three languages. Three. Read it and weep; I'm basically a genius. Add these three languages to my insane observation skills, above-average IQ, and drop-dead gorgeous looks, and I'm a sextuple threat. And that's not even counting my ability to make boxed mac and cheese and reheat fries to perfection. Espionage was always calling my name!

I don't know if you know this, but Mexico has one of the highest rates of violence against women, manifesting as female homicides, or femicides. Violence against women isn't an isolated deal, however. In fact, indigenous women are always going missing in the United States and Canada. All around the world you'll find victims but very little conversation around the people committing these crimes. My goal was always to use my work to help fight this violence. And when the opportunity to help came my way, I got added to the statistics.

I had spent the night in the city, with big plans to begin changing the world in the morning. Watching from my hotel window as a little girl was rewarded with cotton candy ice cream for promising that she'd maintain straight As for all of second grade. Watching an old man walk his old bulldog up and down the avenue. Watching pinup girls and dapper boys make their way to the ballet, hand in hand. Then leaving the show and testing out dance moves together under lampposts and stoplights.

My nights were often spent like this, watching without the means to participate. I fell in love with the world through glass windows and the little things at the core of humanity. While I worked I couldn't join in on the sweet moments that whispered promises of being alive to my heart. I sometimes grew jealous before remembering that I was working to keep those moments safe.

The next day I boarded a train that would take me on the first leg of my journey to Mexico. I allowed my heart an indulgence, smiling back at the brunette man with a suit and dimples to swoon for. Talking to him was the worst, and final, mistake of my life.

CHAPTER 21

A Kiss To Build A Dream On

This time, when Eloise followed Orella down the stairs, it was not a dream, though the cat still wore its snow-white coat. The cat led her to a sitting room she had never seen. The walls were lined with old books and knickknacks. To the left, a generous fireplace, and directly across from it, on the opposite wall, a large window filtered light in to mimic the sun Eloise had once known. In the center of the room was a plush patterned rug, Ansel's red hair formed a crown around her head where she lay, telling Claudette a story.

Claudette sat draped across a green velvet armchair, cigarette in hand. The scene made Eloise feel nostalgic, for some reason. The kind of lazy Sunday setting that made life worth living. The kind where nothing urgent was said, but the words were important in a much sweeter way.

'Hi!" Eloise said when neither girl noted her entrance.

"Jesus!" Ansel squealed, jumping up from her place on the

floor. "It's like Lilith and Bella designed this house to be able to sneak up on people!"

Claudette leaned over and flicked Ansel's arm.

"Don't mind her, she's a little scaredy-cat."

At this, Orella meowed rather loudly, to remind them of her presence and her un-scaredy-cat attitude.

"We're very excited you're here, love. We were both very upset that we drew the shortest sticks and had to meet with you last." Claudette threw a dramatic hand over her forehead, "I hear we're following up your first time flying–how are we supposed to compete with that!"

"With music, duh," Ansel said, scratching under Orella's chin.

"Oh right, yes. That." Claudette stood from the chair, her red dress falling just above her knees as she walked over to the record player. She removed a vinyl and adjusted some knobs until Louis Armstrong's "Kiss to Build a Dream On" filled the room.

Eloise felt the tension leave her as she pondered the normalcy of this moment. Sitting in a parlor, listening to music with two friends.

"What is it like, being a mother?" Claudette asked.

A very normal moment indeed.

"Sacrificing your entire life for an even better one," Eloise said.

Ansel sighed, "My whole life, I have been scrutinized for not wanting to be a mother, as if it is crazy that maybe, just maybe, a woman does not actually want to sacrifice her entire life."

"Crazy of you indeed my beloved Ansel," Claudette said sarcastically. "I always wanted to get married," she sighed. "Wasn't in the cards for someone in my line of work." Eloise recalled from her first breakfast in the house that Claudette had worked as a spy.

"Getting married was the worst mistake of my life," Eloise said before she'd even identified the words in her mind.

"Oh! Did you remember something?" Ansel questioned.

"No." Eloise sighed. "I don't even remember my husband's name." A laugh escaped her. "But I feel like, clearly, I'm close to something." She could identify nothing about her former partner except a feeling of disgust.

"Hey," Ansel said after a few minutes of music, "does anyone wanna summon a spirit?"

Eloise felt the normalcy slipping away but didn't resent it.

CHAPTER 22

Summoning

"Is this some sort of bad joke where you just call one of the other girls in?" Claudette sighed.

"Yeah, aren't *we* spirits?" Eloise asked.

Ansel responded with a giggle of pure lunacy and called out, loudly, for the rest of the residents to come join them. The girls filed into the sitting room, greeting each other and asking Eloise for updates regarding her memory, to which she had nothing to report. Ansel was eager and herded them into the center of the room to sit in a circle before the fireplace.

"We are summoning a spirit ladies!" Ansel announced.

"Finally!" Kali shrieked. "As a horror enthusiast, I've been waiting for this moment my entire life." The girls laughed as Kali and Ansel began barking out instructions: Tala and Eloise were to gather all the candles, Claudette was to set the music, Lulu needed to draw the blinds, and Advaita went to fetch some snacks, because, "summoning makes a girl peckish, duh."

. . .

It was only after Kali had set and lit all the candles in front of them that Eloise began to question what they were doing. Advaita seemed to read her mind, voicing her concerns.

"Ansel, what the fuck are we doing?"

"Summoning," she replied steadily.

"I think everyone just wants to know who, or what, we're summoning. Given that, you know, we ourselves are already dead," Tala said.

"Would y'all just hush up 'n' trust her?" Lulu said. "I actually . . . have done this with her before, that night the rest of y'all went to sleep, a few weeks before Eloise arrived."

Gasps sounded all across the room.

"Traitors!" Claudette said jokingly. Advaita huffed her agreement.

"Summoning spirits is *obviously* an activity you wake up your girls for!" Kali said, offended. Tala and Eloise just laughed.

Lulu swatted the air as if shooing their comments away, "Well we're *trying* to make up for it now!"

"All right." Tala said, "Tell us what we need to do."

As Ansel instructed, the girls sat around the candle cluster in the middle, holding hands in silence, focusing on the foreign words coming out of Ansel's mouth.

And just like that, the energy in the room shifted to a very playful one. It started slowly, just one wisp of coloring whipping past Eloise's cheek, until it filled up every space. The whole room was speckled with fast-moving orbs of floating colors, turning the room into a kaleidoscope of patterns as the multicolored spirits ducked and bobbed around the room. Sprites of every hue were there: fiery red to moody purple, passionate pink to sparkle gold. The women were mesmerize.

"Flower spirits," Kali gasped, eyes full of wonder that mirrored Eloise's, and the rest of the girls.

They got up and danced with the small sprites and each other, smiling and singing and gliding around the floor.

Eloise found herself in a trance, staring at the colors as her brain tried frantically to make sense of the patterns they made in the air.

The movements the spirits were making, or the color combination, or simply just fate, unlocked something in Eloise's mind as she watched the them, and she finally launched back into her memories.

CHAPTER 23

Soul stories: Who are you?

ELOISE

I must have been in denial, not to have seen it sooner. Maybe it was out of a selfish love for my life, or to protect my daughter, namesake of her father, Thomas.

I think of everything that led me to this moment. Visiting Kyoto with my parents and meeting Thomas–a man who traveled everywhere, from India to Mexico, for work. Falling madly in love with him, and feeling inspired to paint for the first time in years. How that inspiration had begun my career. The decision to move in with him, marry him, have a child with him, and name her after him.

How blind have I been?

My hands shake with the realization that my husband is a killer. I can't really process it, truly. My husband? Charismatic, loving, devoted Thomas? A killer?

But the evidence is laid out in front of me; stashes of weapons, Polaroids of his abuse, videos of his rape.

All labeled. Tracking the victims he had come across during each work trip.

. . .

Tala Arrow in California
   Lulu White in Georgia
   Advaita Bedi in Rajasthan
   Kali Omari in New York
   Ansel Walsh in Ireland
   Claudette Cruz in Mexico

I try not to scream. I think of the women, with lives and hearts that will be reduced down to true crime plots and joke punchlines. I think of my daughter, safe at my mom and dad's house.

I think of my husband. Did he call me after these monstrous acts? Ask me how my day was? Did he tell me he missed me?

Was it my fault? Could I have saved these women? I try not to scream as I pick up the phone to call the police, but suddenly he's there. He's caught me catching him. And I can see it in his eyes. The moment he decides I will be his next victim.

CHAPTER 24

The Awakening

Eloise gasped for air as she fell out of her trance, feeling like she'd been dunked under boiling water.

Rage did not begin to encompass the feeling that invaded every space in her body. She felt murderous. He had beaten, raped, and killed the women she had come to love so dearly.

The women who had helped her find herself, held her pain like their own, braided her hair, taught her to fly, and sat with her in the hurt.

And then he did it to her.

And she would make him pay.

Eloise looked around to see the women who had circled around her, and she nodded once before walking outside.

✦+ ° ✦ ·. ✩ .· ✦° +✦

It was the power of sheer rage, unlocked from some long-smoldering cabinet in the women's souls, that allowed them to fly back to the Earth in their winged forms.

• • •

It was the power of them united together that allowed them to manifest temporarily in a physical form on Earth. The sight of them, disheveled from flight and burning with anger, scared the man half to death, starting their job for them.

It was the power that only the thirst for revenge can supply that allowed their weapons to break into him, instead of going through him like a ghost is supposed to.

It was the power of women that ended the man.

CHAPTER 25

Lilith

I didn't cry when the man died.

No, I threw my head back and cackled in the shadows of the room where I'd once wept for Eloise.

Death had hung like an unanswered question in the air for days, frequently summoning me to the room before it was truly time. I watched as the man clung to his life, as blood was drawn, and as the dead women inflicted a fraction of what he deserved onto him.

After the final strings of his life came untwined, I charred his soul to ash and brought it home.

The revenge seared into his essence made for excellent nightshade fertilizer.

CHAPTER 26

Sunday Paper Horoscope

Eloise had never paid much mind to the constellations and their alleged shapes. She had always admired them, but never felt called to trace invisible lines like connect the dots or learn the names given to them by old astronomers that were surely dust now. But as she stood on Earth for the last time and looked out upon the stars, she closed her eyes and tried to recall the coffee-stained Sunday paper and how her father would give it to her when he was done reading so she could look at the pictures in the horoscope column.

She supposed that if she squinted her eyes really hard and summoned some child-like imagination, maybe what Ansel pointed at could be mistaken for the shape of a lion. If the person mistaken had never seen a lion. Or any mammal for that matter.

Any doubt was seized from Eloise's mind when all around her, the stars began to shift. They came into focus like a pop-up book, from 2D to 3D in one turn of a page, or blink of an eye. Merged, the constellations materialized onto the ground with the girls. Standing in front of them were pure stars taking the forms of a lion, bull, scorpion, chameleon, and more, ready to transport the women back to Lilith's Haven through the Milky Way.

She thought on the ride back. About the women she was flying with and how they had known who her husband was and helped her heal anyway. Had loved her, despite. She smiled at the thought of them and what they had just done together. Eloise might be dead, but her soul still lived on. The same could not be said for her late husband.

CHAPTER 27

Lilith returns

The women came home to find Lilith, returned from her work as a reaperess. They ran towards her in greeting. Eloise hung back, not yet having met Lilith beyond a dream. But as soon as the rest of the girls backed away, Lilith swept Eloise up into a warm, motherly embrace.

"Welcome home!" Lilith said.

"I could say the same to you." Eloise smiled. "We have much to discuss."

Eloise found herself sitting at the same table where she had opened Lilith's letter. Only this time instead of the letter, it was the writer herself.

CHAPTER 28

Lilith

"I saw you in my dream," Eloise said, eyes wide with clarity. "Among the nightshades. Why do you have so many?"

I thought of mud. I smiled.

"To poison God."

Eloise grinned.

"How many plants do you have?"

"100,005."

"How many do you need to kill him?"

"100,006."

Eloise immediately stood up "I have mine! From my arrival. It's in my room I'll go get it-"

I gently grabbed her wrist before she could leave.

"I need you to understand the consequences, Eloise," I said

"Oh, okay," she replied, sitting back down.

I took a deep breath, preparing the same speech I had given to 100,005 other brave women before Eloise.

"God has the power, you know. To stop men from killing and raping, but he doesn't. He still rewards them in the afterlife, if they pray hard enough." Eloise looked disgusted, but not surprised.

"One hundred thousand and six. That's how many night-shades I need, but they must come from souls fixed on revenge. I have a plan. To poison him. But there is a catch. Should I fail, he will know. He will know the soul behind every single leaf and berry that tried to kill him, and he will damn you all. And I wouldn't be around to stop him, Eloise."

Determination glinted in Eloise's eyes as she left the room. The look was still fixed in her eyes minutes later when she returned, purple plant in hand.

CHAPTER 29

Lilith

It took days. To bathe in the belladonna. To infuse it into my black lipstick, my perfume, my hair. To bake the poison into God's favorite feast. To concentrate it into wine. The girls helped; Bella did the most. Orella followed me everywhere, her coat black and her eyes ever watching.

It wasn't hard to get him to invite me into his palace, God loves any offer of repentance. I brought over his favorite meal and bit my tongue when a joke about murderous women in the kitchen crossed my mind. He devoured the poison unknowingly, all the while breathing in my scent and my empty apology.

It wasn't hard to seduce him after the meal–he is a man, at the end of the day. He underestimated me like they all do, so caught up in my beauty that they never even think of my mind. It was the kiss of my black lipstick that finally sent him to death.

I buried him outside his palace, in the mud.

CHAPTER 30

Lilith Takes the Throne

Nestled between the constellations, atop a cliff made of ever-flowing moonlight, sat a house full of dead women. It was on the porch of that very house that nine women and a cat prepared to leave. It was bittersweet, leaving the home. Sweet, the healing they and countless others had done there. Bitter, the reason why.

They had important places to be now, a universe to rule over with love, replacing the violence that had been. A party was being held tonight, at the palace where the old king had once lived. Every woman who had taken a risk to end his reign was invited, and all 100,006 of them showed up.

In pale, draped dresses the women danced together. Each had her own mask for the occasion. A few hung a crescent moon from their face, some opted for an animal–a fox or a lion. Among the most complimented were those that mimicked a belladonna plant.

· · ·

But every mask was shed so that Lilith could see their smiles as she took the throne and inherited the power to change the world.

A task they would embark on, all of them, together.

So that one day, no dead women would need Lilith's Haven ever again.

A Note On A Pandemic

While this story is fictitious, violence against women is not. In fact, violence against women is, according to the World Health Organization, a global public health pandemic. You would think when an issue warrants the title "global public health pandemic" more people would talk about it. More people would take a stand against rape culture. More people would shut down unfunny jokes. More people would raise their children to understand consent, but here we are. I honestly don't know the solution, there is a lot of work that needs to be done, but I think it starts with education and a conversation. I believe part of the erasure of this issue is because it's so diverse. It affects trans women, gay women, women of color, disabled women, and people have a hard time with intersectional issues that don't fit in a singular box. As of right now, this global pandemic feels invisible or undercover, but it's not. It's happening all around. It's in the music we listen to and the media we consume. It's in the way we talk about women and the way we shut them down when they try to speak. It was my sole purpose in writing this book to spark a conversation so that we might begin to see change. We must be courageous in our journey to end this pandemic, standing up to oppressors and bystanders alike, because they really are the same thing. We must be vigilant in our efforts to spread awareness, raise a better generation, and as always, believe survivors regardless of gender. You can learn more about it on the World Health Organization's Website. You can educate yourself on steps to take against gender violence in the UN Women's article titled, "Take action: 10 ways you can help end violence against women." If you your-self have been affected in any way by this violence, know that you are loved, know that it was not your fault, and now that there are resources available to you that you can find on womenshealth.gov.

About the Author

Hi, I'm Reagan! I'm a writing and film major at Savannah College of Art and Design in pursuit of my dreams to become a movie director/author/screenplay writer triple threat. When I'm not reading or writing, you can probably find me at a concert or watching a horror movie. Or listening to the Hamilton soundtrack, but don't tell anyone.

You can find future updates on new projects at reaganellis.org or on my instagram @reaganelliss if you're cool.

Acknowledgments

I am literally so excited to write this page, I have so many people I am grateful for. I think I want to start off by thanking every woman I have ever met, if it's not too ambitious. Women have such a way about them, and our interactions throughout my life have not only shaped me, but this story. The relationships in this story are based on us! We're so magical and healing and impactful and powerful it's crazy. A special thank you to my all time favorite woman, my Mama. The most magical, healing, impactful, powerful, loving, woman ever, the world does not deserve your light. Thank you for being so good at picking friends, and surrounding yourself with outstanding role models during my developmental years, "Aunts" that helped raise me. Heather, Debbie, Jackie, Donna, Dawn, Cindy, to name a few.

To my Dad and Rebekah, for not only assisting me financially in the completion of this book, but for giving me a safe space to find myself and my dreams, allowing room for error and showing me nothing but love along the way. I hope I can one day do something even half as important as that for you.

Alex, thank you for your unwavering support in my writing pursuits. You have no idea how much your texts can make my day and encourage me to keep going even from miles and miles away. I love you forever, you win the world's best brother every time.

Kit, you've been telling me stories and encouraging me to do the same my entire life. As in all of our writing, there is so much of you, Sam, and me in this book. You are, and always will be, the first to read my work and the last to double and triple check because you care so much. You are my number one supporter and I will never be able to properly thank you for that.

Sam, my roommate for this endeavor! You were my rock for everything, the good and bad, as I created this. Without you to talk to, Lilith's Haven might've remained unwritten forever.

To the reason the sisters exist, Aunt Deanna and Uncle Greg for always treating me like your own, I have so much love for you four.

Ellora Shah! I can't wait to hug you and thank you for the pure magic you did with this cover. I cannot believe I get to live with someone so beautiful and talented. We're going to have so much fun, I am eager to see what the future holds for us.

To my therapist for girlbossing, Ellen McCanless for beta reading, and Sophia Dembling for editing.

I did in fact save the most important for last. Carmen Lolla, my chosen sister, I have so much I want to immortalize on this page in case you ever need a reminder. Firstly, thank you for being my best friend. It's such a simple sentence, and yet it is one that I do not say enough. When everyone else left, you stayed. When I needed someone to believe in me, you did. When I didn't want to live anymore, you reminded me why I should stick around. You have shown me what unconditional love looks like, accepting me for who I am. Even when I am a girl screeching along to Glee at 2 AM. I don't know anyone else who would put up with that side of me. Now the hard part. You are not what happened to you. You are a lot of things, sarcastic, witty, intelligent, beautiful, brave, but never that. You blow me away every day in your refusal to stay silent, you give them hell every time, and every time, I am in awe of your courage. You are an inspiration to anyone that has the privilege of knowing you. If you read this and thought Lilith's bad-assery seemed familiar- I got news for you. Your stamp of approval on this project is what made me follow through to the finish line.

And to close this out I have the opposite of an acknowledgement. To all the Thomas' of the world, a big fat fuck you. I hope you have an awful time suffering in that special pocket of hell that is 100,006 degrees hotter for eternity. It's what you deserve.

www.ingramcontent.com/pod-product-compliance
Lightning Source LLC
Chambersburg PA
CBHW021559310726
48972CB00003B/869